MORRIS'S
DISAPPEARING BAG

ROSEMARY WELLS

Viking

VIKING
Published by the Penguin Group
Penguin Putnam Books for Young Readers, 345 Hudson Street, New York, New York 10014, U.S.A.
Penguin Books Ltd, 27 Wrights Lane, London W8 5TZ, England
Penguin Books Australia Ltd, Ringwood, Victoria, Australia
Penguin Books Canada Ltd, 10 Alcorn Avenue, Toronto, Ontario, Canada M4V 3B2
Penguin Books (N.Z.) Ltd, 182-190 Wairau Road, Auckland 10, New Zealand

Penguin Books Ltd, Registered Offices: Harmondsworth, Middlesex, England

First published in 1975 by The Dial Press

This edition with new illustrations published in 1999 by Viking,
a division of Penguin Putnam Books for Young Readers.

3   5   7   9   10   8   6   4   2

The Library of Congress has catalogued the Dial edition as follows:
Wells, Rosemary.
Morris's disappearing bag.
[1.Christmas stories.] I. Title.
PZ7.W46843Mo [E] 75-9202
ISBN 0-8037-5441-8 ISBN 0-8037-5510-4 lib. bdg.

Viking edition ISBN 0-670-88721-8

Printed in Hong Kong
Set in Minister

TO VICTORIA

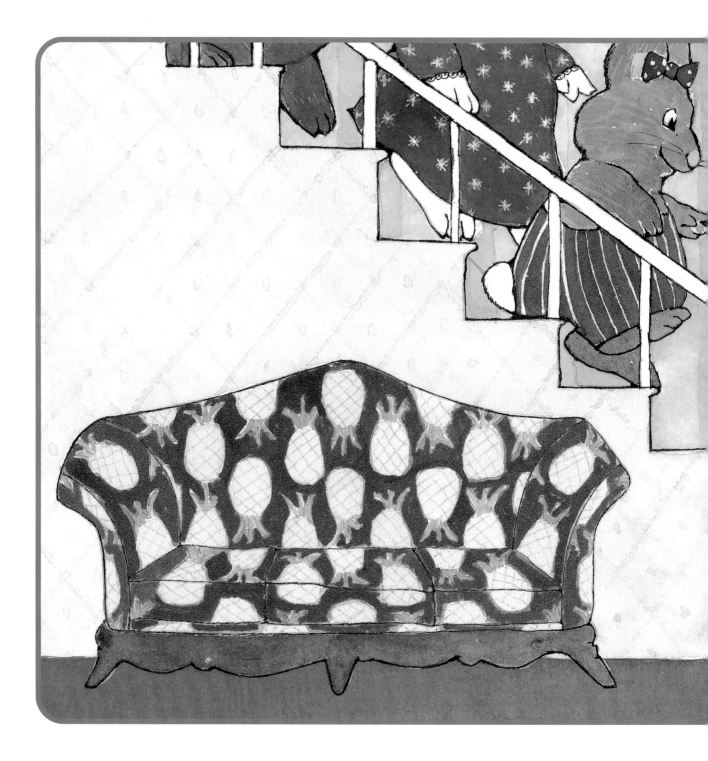

It was Christmas morning.
"Wow!" said Morris.

Morris's brother, Victor,
got a hockey outfit.

Morris's sister, Rose,
got a beauty kit.

Morris's other sister, Betty,
got a chemistry set.

And Morris got a bear.

All Christmas day Victor played hockey
and Rose made herself beautiful
and Betty mixed acids.

And then Betty made herself beautiful
and Victor sorted test tubes
and Rose played left wing.

And then Victor made himself beautiful
and Betty played goalie
and Rose invented a new gas.

Morris was too young to play
with chemicals, said Betty,
he might blow up the house.

He was too little to play hockey,
said Victor, he might get hurt.

And he was too silly to use the
beauty kit, said Rose, he would
waste all the lipstick.

Nobody wanted Morris's bear.

"Come," said Morris's mother,
"let's make a hat for your bear."

"No!" said Morris.

"Let's take your bear for a walk,"
suggested Morris's father.
"No!" said Morris.

Morris wouldn't eat his dinner.
"What's the matter with Morris?" asked his father.
"I think he hit himself with the hockey puck,"
said Victor.

"Maybe he ate the lipstick," said Rose.
"It was the gas," said Betty.
"He breathed it in."

Morris sat under the Christmas tree.

Suddenly he noticed a package that
had been overlooked.

He opened it.
In it was a Disappearing Bag.

Morris crawled right in.

"Morris?" said Victor.
"Right here," said Morris.
"Where?" asked Victor.

"Where's Morris?" asked Betty and Rose.
"Over here," said Morris.

But they couldn't find him.
"Maybe he blew himself up," said Betty.

"Do you suppose he's so beautiful we wouldn't recognize him?" asked Rose. "Dad!" shouted Victor, "Morris is skating so fast we can't see him."

Morris came out of his bag.
"Where were you?" asked Victor.
"I was in my Disappearing Bag,"
said Morris.

"I want to use it," shouted Victor.

"Me first," said Rose.

"You can use my chemicals," said Betty.

Morris held open his bag.
Everybody disappeared at once.

Then he zoomed

and mixed

and beautified

until bedtime.

"Bedtime!" said Morris.

"May I use the bag tomorrow?"
asked Rose.
"I want to sleep in it tonight,"
said Betty.

"Morris," said Victor, "I hope you
remember where you put the bag."

But Morris was already fast asleep.